SAGA OF THE

Mary Celeste

An Ill-Fated
MYSTERY SHIP

The Saga of the
Mary Celeste

ILL-FATED
MYSTERY SHIP

Stanley T. Spicer

Nimbus Publishing Limited
PO Box 9166
Halifax, NS B3K 5M8
(902) 455-4286
www.nimbus.ns.ca

Printed and bound in Canada

National Library of Canada Cataloguing in Publication

Spicer, Stanley T., 1924-
Saga of the Mary Celeste : ill-fated mystery ship / Stanley T. Spicer.

Includes bibliographical references.
ISBN 1-55109-402-9
(Previously published by Lancelot Press: ISBN 0-88999-546-x)

1. Mary Celeste (Brig) I. Title.

G530.M3574S6 2002 910.4'5 C2002-901523-5

We acknowledge the financial support of the Government of Canada through the Book Publishing Industry Development Program (BPIDP) and the Canada Council for our publishing activities.

❖ *Contents* ❖

The *Mary Celeste* as she appeared when first sighted by the *Dei Gratia*, December, 1872 from a wood engraving by Rudolph Ruzicka.
Courtesy of Peabody Museum of Salem.

❖ Foreword ❖

Joseph Conrad, the seaman and author of another time, once wrote:

> The ocean has the conscienceless temper of a savage autocrat spoiled by much adulation. He cannot brook the slightest appearance of defiance, and has remained the irreconcilable enemy of ships and men ever since ships and men had the unheard-of audacity to go afloat together in the face of his frown.

The sea is a body of contrasting moods. If in one moment it can elicit rapturous responses as sunlight dances on its wavelets or the moon casts a bright path across its darkened surface, at other times it can be vicious. In its fury it tears away land, topples shore-side buildings and sweeps living things into its maw.

Those who venture on or under the sea do so at risk. Upwards of one hundred sailing vessels built around the Bay of Fundy and its rivers vanished, disappeared without a trace. What happened will never be known for the sea rarely gives up its secrets. Hundreds of other vessels encountering the ocean's wrath sank or were driven ashore on some exposed coast. Occasionally the sea can be forgiving. In December 1879 the ship *County of Pictou* was sailing from England towards Philadelphia when a storm beat down. A huge wave washed two sailors, Peter Carroll and Murdock Morrison, overboard. A following wave washed them back on board the ship.

The sea has spawned tales of the supernatural, of ghost ships, phantom ships and of the sudden appearance of sailors centuries-old. Yet perhaps the most enduring mystery relating to the sea concerns a small Nova Scotia-built brigantine. The vessel's career spanned twenty-four years and they were years of almost continuous misfortune highlighted by the sudden disappearance of all on board. It is a mystery that can never really be solved. It is the story of the *Mary Celeste*.

Stanley T. Spicer

Spencers Island, N.S.

❖ Acknowledgements ❖

In addition to the sources listed in the bibliography I am grateful to the following for their assistance with this work:

Dr. Charles Armour, Archivist, Dalhousie University Library, Halifax
Nova Scotia Public Archives, Halifax
Peabody Museum of Salem, Salem, Massachusetts
Ernest E. Coates, R.R. 2, Nappan, N.S.
D. Rhodes Dewis, Parrsboro, N.S.
Mrs. Hilda Fletcher, Advocate Harbour, N.S.
Mrs. Augusta Morris, Advocate Harbour, N.S.
and as always to my wife Gwen.

Spencer's Island beach where the Amazon was launched in 1861. The mill marks the site of the old shipyard. A post World War I photo. *Courtesy of the author.*

❖ 1 ❖

Where the Story Began

On the beach at Spencers Island, a small community some forty kilometers west of Parrsboro, Nova Scotia, a stone cairn bears this inscription,

> Nearby the world's most famous mystery ship, the *Mary Celeste*, a brigantine was built and launched in 1861. Was first named the *Amazon*. In 1868 she was driven ashore in a storm and after being repaired was renamed the *Mary Celeste*. In December 1872 she was discovered at sea with all sail set and everything in order but not a person was on board or ever found.

The *Mary Celeste* was a small vessel born on the north side of Minas Channel in the upper reaches of the Bay of Fundy. In size, rig and design she differed not at all from hundreds of others of her type built in Nova Scotia during the middle years of the nineteenth century. Yet this one was destined to gain worldwide fame because of the disappearance of her company. Books, magazine and newspaper articles, authors like A. Conan Doyle, the creator of Sherlock Holmes, and in later years radio and television programs have all fed on the mystery. Even Hollywood came out with a movie version of the incident. The full story of the *Mary Celeste* is much more than the one voyage in which she carried all on board to oblivion. The brigantine attracted misfortune from her first voyage to her last and there were many who came to call her 'bewitched' and a 'hoodoo vessel.'

The fact that this little vessel was found sailing alone and unmanned was not in itself all that unusual during the age of sail. In one short period alone, from 1887 to 1893 inclusive, the American Hydrographic Office reported 1,628 known derelicts, an average of 232 per year or nineteen each month. The reasons for their abandonment varied but always human judgement was involved. In one common scenario a vessel survives a storm but is extensively damaged and is considered unseaworthy by those on board. At the first opportunity a passing ship is signalled, the men are taken off leaving the abandoned vessel to continue on her uncertain way. However, in this situation the fate of the officers and crew becomes known, unlike the fate of those on board the *Mary Celeste.*

Ten persons were on board the *Celeste* and ten persons vanished; this is the basis for the mystery. And it was fueled by the lengthy hearings which followed in Gibraltar complete with insinuations of murder, revenge and conspiracies. That the more gory theories proved untrue seemed to matter little. Most were repeated time and again.

The *Mary Celeste* story had its beginnings in the early 1860s in the small neighboring communities of Spencers Island and Advocate in western Cumberland County. They are situated in an area rich in history and encompassing some of the finest scenery in Nova Scotia. To seaward the two communities are separated by majestic Cape D'Or where Prince Henry Sinclair of the Orkney Islands may have wintered nearly a full century before the epic voyage of Christopher Columbus. West of Advocate are thousands of acres of unoccupied land reaching to the tip of Cape Chignecto and destined to become Nova Scotia's largest wilderness park.

Today the main road through these two communities is

lined with neat, wooden homes, mostly painted white and some displaying lines, buoys, traps and other paraphernalia of the fishing trade. The area has a doctor, a new hospital, a volunteer fire department and a district school which along with a senior citizens' complex are all located in Advocate. The newly rebuilt wharf in Advocate is crowded with fishing craft which pursue lobsters and scallops. In Spencers Island the local store has operated in the same building since the halcyon days of shipbuilding. The nearby lighthouse, once a sentinel for busy traffic on the Bay of Fundy, now serves as a small pictorial museum.

These days there are few reminders of the years when Spencers Island and Advocate together launched some 150 sailing vessels. The shipyards have disappeared and most of the wharves along the shore have fallen into decay. No more do dozens of schooners and square-riggers anchor off Spencers Island waiting for a favorable wind. No longer are the gypsum barges, those cut down old square-riggers loaded with raw gypsum from the Windsor area, towed to Spencers Island and hooked up to ocean-going tugs for the longer passage to New York. Only some large old houses remain as mementos of the men who built and sailed their windships to ports all over the world. Those and a cemetery on a hill in Advocate in which numerous stones bear the brief epitaph, 'Lost At Sea.'

The last farmhouse west of Advocate Harbor and adjoining the wilderness area of Cape Chignecto sits on land that once belonged to Joshua Dewis. And without Joshua Dewis it is unlikely there would have been a *Mary Celeste*. Dewis was born at Economy, Nova Scotia in 1815. The Napoleonic Wars had just ended and times were hard. In those early years of the nineteenth century the only practical way to travel from the north shore of Minas Basin and Cobequid Bay to the markets in Windsor was by water. As a young man Dewis took note and began to build small boats for local farmers to transport their produce to market. Gradually he began to build larger boats and about 1845 he launched a schooner. Sometime later, for the exact date is obscure, he moved to West Advocate and purchased a farm with a large timber tract. While other factors may have influenced his move from Economy there is little doubt that Dewis foresaw a bright future for shipbuilding in the Spencers Island-Advocate area.

Even so Dewis would not be fulfilling the role of a shipbuilding pioneer in his new location. Recorded shipbuilding had been underway in Advocate at least since 1816 when John Loomer launched the ninety-one ton schooner *Rachel.* Prior to 1861, when Dewis would launch his brigantine at Spencers Island, over 180 vessels had already been built in Parrsboro and west along the shore and of these at least forty-four had been launched in Advocate.

On the provincial scene the 1860s were years in which shipbuilding in Nova Scotia underwent a rather spectacular growth helping substantially to place Canada among the leading shipbuilding and shipowning nations of the world. The growth was marked not only by the numbers of vessels produced but also by their increased size. Prior to 1860 the average size of vessels built in Nova Scotia yards barely exceed 100 tons and few exceeded 1,000 tons. Thereafter the size of vessels increased marketly and in 1874, when 175 vessels were built in the province, the average size was over 480 tons. It was in this year that the largest of them all, the full-rigged ship *W.D. Lawrence* of 2,459 tons was launched at Maitland.

Over the years some authors of *Mary Celeste* stories have tended to picture the place of her origin as 'a remote and primitive district.' It was hardly that. The census figures taken on March 30, 1861 for Nova Scotia were based on the eleven polling districts in the province of which Advocate was one. In that year the provincial population totalled 330,875 while that of Cumberland County registered 19,533. Within the Advocate polling district, which included Spencers Island, there resided 567 males and 507 females for a total of 1,074 persons and among them were 181 families. Their occupations included farmers, farm laborers, mariners, lumbermen, carpenters and joiners, shipwrights, seamstresses, blacksmiths, shoemakers, teachers, a tanner, lighthouse keeper, a cooper, clockmaker and a doctor. A 'remote and primitive district' indeed!

By the middle years of the nineteenth century the Advocate-Spencers Island area had long been inhabited. Indians had encamped there and the French had farmed and built dykes in Advocate and had settled on Cape D'Or where they remained until the expulsion in 1755. A group of Scots had also settled on Cape D'Or about 1765 but their settlement was shortlived. After suffering many hardships they moved away, many apparently going to Antigonish County. When the Loyalists arrived in the 1780s they founded the settlements we know today.

Even the place names are old. Advocate is derived from the original name Avocat said to have been bestowed by Champlain. The English name Advocate predates the Loyalists as Advocate Harbour appears on land maps prepared by the provincial land surveyor, Charles Morris, in 1767. The Indian name for Spencers Island was Wochuk meaning a small kettle or pot. According to the late C. Bruce Fergusson, former provincial archivist, Spencers Island was named in honor of Lord Spencer and was appearing as early as 1714-15 on Nathaniel Blackmore's chart.

In the early years of settlement the sea was the main highway and there was much traffic back and forth across the Bay of Fundy. One reason was that the major markets were on the south side of the bay. Then until 1840 Parrsborough Township which included Spencers Island and Advocate was part of Kings County and after 1829 Kentville was the shiretown. Residents of the Parrsboro shore who did not have their own means of crossing the bay could journey to Parrsboro where a packet service had operated between Parrsboro and Windsor since the late 1700s.

Another important ingredient to civilized life along the shore came early in the form of a postal service. A post office has been established in Parrsboro about 1812 and in Advocate in 1836. Spencers Island was awarded a postal way station in 1870 and W.H. Bigelow, proprietor of the local general store, was appointed the first postmaster.

The method of delivering the mail along the shore was dictated by the state of the roads. In the early years of the nineteenth century, when the roads were little more than paths through the woods, the mails were carried on horseback. However, by the mid 1860s roads had improved and the horse and carriage had come into use in summer and the horse and sleigh in winter. But always weather was a determining factor and mail delivery was rather haphazard until relatively recent years.

The means of providing a formal education to children also appeared early in these pioneer settlements. The first school in Advocate evidently opened its doors in 1820 with a Mr. Dormandy as teacher. By 1859 James McCabe was the teacher and in addition to the 3Rs he was providing instruction in music, astronomy and navigation. Many a young man intent on becoming an officer on board ship began his required studies into the complexities of navigation under the watchful eye of Mr. McCabe. In 1865 the Inspector of Schools for Cumberland County was able to report that the Advocate Superior School, James McCabe, Principal, had registered eighty-two pupils and 'it was the only school in Cumberland County teaching military drill.'

The first recorded school in Spencers Island was established in 1848. Local history suggests that it was over the store operated by Daniel Cox and his brother-in-law W.H. Payzant in a building later used as the shipyard cookhouse. By the time Joshua Dewis was building his brigantine on the beach it is quite probable that Miss Laura Cox was teaching in a school building located near the present church.

The church in its various denominations always played a vital role in the lives of the earlier inhabitants and it is recorded that over the years Roman Catholics, Methodists, Anglicans, Presbyterians and Baptists were all represented by the residents in the Spencers Island-Advocate district.

For several generations the religious needs of the people were served by circuit ministers or by clergymen who travelled to the area when they could and how they could. Since Joshua Dewis and his wife Naomi were lifelong Baptists it may be worthy of note that the Baptist congregation was formally organized in 1840. Just when their first church was erected is not known but minutes for the year 1865 note 'the need to have the meeting house painted.' Obviously the facility had been in use for some years prior to that time.

Thus by 1860 when Dewis was completing his plans to build a vessel, the Spencers Island-Advocate area was well-settled; its inhabitants were farming, lumbering and building vessels. The 'remote and primitive district' was in reality peopled by resourceful, independent men and women with a strong faith in their present and in their future.

Spencer's Island beach. The schooner on the stocks marks the site of the old shipyard

❖ 2 ❖

A Brigantine Named Amazon

Later Renamed Mary Celeste

There were undoubtedly several factors influencing Joshua Dewis' decision to build the brigantine in Spencers Island. The beach area there was an ideal site for the shipyard he had in mind and certainly there was an abundance of raw materials within easy reach. Then there were family relationships. The two largest landowners in the settlement were the Spicer brothers, Isaac and Jacob. Jacob's wife Mary, and Joshua's wife, Naomi, were the daughters of George Reid, an Advocate farmer and a promised investor in the project. And Joshua's son, Robert, would marry Isaac's daughter, Emily Jane, a month after the launching of the vessel. Thus there were relatives who could not only provide timber for the vessel, they would also invest in her.

During the age of sail most vessels built in the Maritime provinces were financed and owned on the basis of sixty-four equal shares. While one person or a firm might own a vessel outright, it was a more usual practice for the shares to be spread among several owners. Thus losses — and profits — were divided among a number of persons. It was also more likely that an individual would own some shares in several vessels rather than own one vessel outright. So, in 1860 as Dewis began to build the brigantine, the first shareholders were:

Joshua Dewis, master builder	16 shares
W.H. Bigelow, Daniel Cox, W.H. Payzant, local businessmen	12 shares
Jacob Spicer, farmer and lumberman	8 shares
Isaac Spicer, farmer and lumberman	8 shares
George Reid, farmer and lumberman	8 shares
William Thompson, Economy, rigger	8 shares
Robert McLellan, the vessel's first captain	4 shares

The keel for the vessel was laid in the fall of 1860. There is no known record of a mill in Spencers Island at the time which meant that all the timber had to be squared and shaped by hand using saw, broad axe and adze. And all of the planks and boards had to be cut individually using a sawpit. The timber to be sawn was placed over a deep pit with one man standing on top of the timber and another below in the pit, between them working a long saw through the timber. The man below, the pit sawyer, had the toughest job in the shipyard working all day below ground level, arms upraised and sawdust raining down on him.

The other shipyard facilities were minimal. Dewis built a small building to house the carpenters' benches and the yard tools. He provided a forge for ironwork and a wood-fired steambox to soften the planks for bending. These and a rough shed to house the fittings and supplies needed for the vessel comprised the entire shipyard. The vessel was built in the open subject to all the vagaries of the weather. The facility was typical of the small shipyards of the time and in those years they could be found just about anywhere a new vessel could be floated. Only in the more elaborate yards were there lofts where full-sized plans of the vessel's component parts could be laid down on the floor, where a building housed the carver who turned out the figurehead, wheel and sternboards. Only in the

Brigantine *Amazon*, later the mystery vessel *Mary Celeste* launched May, 1861, Spencers Island, Nova Scotia.
Courtesy New Brunswick Museum

larger yards were there accommodations for the workers to eat and sleep, a sawmill, joiner's shop and a yard office. Few Maritime builders cut and sewed their own sails, these were turned out by specialists in a few of the larger shipbuilding centres.

By the time the winter of 1860-61 had set in Dewis' new vessel was 'in frame,' that is the keel was laid, the stem, sternpost and frames or ribs were all shaped and fastened in place. Thus she was left for the winter months, a time for the green timbers to season before the planking went on. The shipwrights went home but Dewis and the Spicer brothers used the winter months to search out the right timber and bring it to the shipyard for finishing off the vessel in the spring.

It is unlikely that Dewis had any difficulty in selecting the brigantine rig. In those days it was considered one of the handiest of rigs for smaller vessels with square sails set on the foremast and fore and aft sails on the mainmast. A competent captain and five or six men could take a brigantine anywhere and her rig combined the best sailing qualities of both the square-rigger and the schooner.

When the warmer days of spring arrived the shipwrights resumed work on the vessel. After the hull planking had been sawn, holes were bored with augers for the treenails, the round fastenings that held the planking in place. The treenails, or trunnels, were often cut out of hackmatack, beech or other hardwoods. They were slightly larger in diameter at one end and when driven home and the ends sawn off flush, the inner end was split and wedged. When the treenails became wet they swelled and provided a tight fastening.

After the hull planking was in place and the vessel salted, that is rock salt packed in every place where wood met wood to discourage rot, the caulkers went to work. They drove strands of oakum into every seam in the hull and on deck and then payed the seams with hot pitch. As the work of finishing the hull went on the masts were fashioned and stepped. Then the riggers took over and began the work of arranging the intricate web of rigging which supported the masts and spars and controlled the sails. The sails, probably cut and sewn by sailmakers in Halifax or Windsor, were bent on, the necessary equipment for the vessel placed on board including anchors, spare sails and cordage, compass, a small boat and the brigantine was ready for launching.

The vessel was launched on May 18, 1861 and for reasons known only to himself, Joshua Dewis named her *Amazon.* Years later when some of the large vessels were launched at Spencers Island it was not uncommon for a thousand or more people to come for 'the launch.' They came from up and down the shore, from Amherst and Truro and according to one contemporary description, 'every yard for two miles in either direction of the shipyard was filled with visiting horses and wagons or carriages.' And they came in boats small and large from Canning, Kingsport, Windsor and from communities on the other side of Minas Channel. A great throng had a great time and the inevitable tea meeting enriched local coffers for another good cause.

It is unlikely that the launching of the *Amazon* attracted such a crowd. There would have been a celebration of sorts for launchings were almost always celebrated but this one was probably much more local in scope. Years later, some writers in describing the trials and tribulations of the vessel indicated that she stuck on the ways. This may have been intended to add another incident to the misfortunes of the vessel but it was always emphatically denied by George D. Spicer — and he was launched on her.

According to her first register the brigantine measured out at 198.42 gross tons. She was 99.3 feet in length, 25.5 feet in breadth and her depth was 11.7 feet. The vessel had a square stern, one deck and had fore and aft cabins. A mixture of birch, beech and maple was used in the hull below the light load-line and spruce from there to the rails. She was registered in Parrsboro, the nearest port of registry, on June 10, 1861. Although there are no known figures on the cost of building the brigantine, two years later, in 1863, she was valued at $4,600.

The launching of the *Amazon* marked the beginning of the shipbuilding industry in Spencers Island. In the years to come nearly thirty square-riggers and schooners would be constructed in the local yard. If the settlement was not noted for the numbers of vessels it produced, it was noted for the size, quality and performance of many of these vessels. Some like the barque *J.F. Whitney* and the ship *E.J. Spicer* became well known for fast passages. Others like the ships *Stephen D. Horton, Charles S. Whitney* and *George T. Hay* all exceeded 1,600 tons, among the larger Maritime vessels of their time, while the ship *Glooscap* at 1,734 tons was the largest sailing vessel built in Cumberland County.

Once afloat the *Amazon* sailed up the Bay of Fundy to Five Islands, N.S. to load lumber for London. Her master, Robert McLellan of nearby Economy, had been recently married and while the vessel was loading he was far from well. However, McLellan was determined to make the voyage perhaps thinking the fresh sea air would help improve his health. The brigantine finished loading and cleared Five Islands for London. She was still in the Bay when McLellan developed pneumonia. The mate put the vessel about and sailed back to Spencers Island. The stricken captain was taken to Jacob Spicer's home where he died a few hours later. The next day some of the crew including young George Spicer wrapped the body in a blanket, placed it in the *Amazon's* boat and sailed to Economy. As they approached the shore the sailors saw McLellan's young bride come running to learn why they had returned. It was a sight Spicer never forgot.

The new captain of the *Amazon* was Captain John (Jack) Parker of Walton, Nova Scotia who would take her to London. That voyage was later described by Robert Dewis, Joshua's son, who like George Spicer had been launched on the vessel and was a member of the crew on her first voyage:

> We started on the voyage again (after McLellan's death) and for some reason I cannot recall we put into Eastport, Maine. On the way out of port we ran into some fish weirs

> in the Narrows and then lay for some days before we finally proceeded on our course across the Atlantic. We got to London, discharged the cargo and loaded another for Lisbon. On the way down the channel we ran into an English brig in the Strait of Dover and sunk her quickly, the crew climbing on board with us and all being saved. We put into Dover and landed our shipwrecks, repaired damages and resumed our voyage.

Within months of her launch the brigantine had lost her first captain and sunk another vessel. Her star-crossed career was truly underway.

Over the next few years the *Amazon* sailed between various ports in the Mediterranean, the British Isles and the West Indies. Robert Dewis stayed with the vessel for two years and during this time George Spicer came back to the vessel and sailed as mate for just over two years. He was mate when the brigantine was in Progreso, Mexico and word was received of the assassination of President Abraham Lincoln on April 14, 1865.

In the early fall of 1867 the brigantine brought a cargo of corn into Halifax from Baltimore and Spicer left the vessel. After discharging the corn the *Amazon* sailed in ballast to load coal at Big Glace Bay, Cape Breton. According to Robert Dewis the vessel was anchored in the harbor when a gale sprang up and drove the vessel on shore just where an American company was excavating for a dock.

The *Amazon* suffered severe damage and now her story becomes somewhat murky. According to some accounts the insurance on her did not cover the Cape Breton coast in the fall months and her owners could not afford the expense of refloating and undertaking the necessary repairs. At this point a notation was made in her registry at Parrsboro:

> The above-named vessel (*Amazon*) was wrecked at Big Glace Bay, C.B. and registered at the Port of Sydney the 9th November, 1867. Old certificate cancelled and

returned to this office. Registry closed (in Parrsboro) 18th November, 1867.

The change in registry from Parrsboro to Sydney was due to the fact that one Alexander McBean of Big Glace Bay became sole owner of the wreck and then immediately sold the vessel to John H. Beatty of the same place.

Little is known of the vessel until November 1868 when she was auctioned off in New York to Captain Richard W. Haines for the sum of $1,750. Somehow he managed to procure an American registry for the brigantine and changed her name to *Mary Celeste*. It was a choice of name with no known origin or derivation.

By now the American Civil War had ended and the economy was suffering. Haines had no luck with the vessel and after about a year she was seized in New York and sold for debt. It was at this point that Captain James H. Winchester enters the picture. He bought the *Mary Celeste* and over the next few years kept her on the West Indies run. By now the vessel was needing repairs and Winchester decided to enlarge her at the same time.

On October 29, 1872 the *Mary Celeste* was in New York preparing for her fateful voyage. A new register had been issued to the vessel listing the following owners:

Captain James H. Winchester, managing owner	12/24 shares
Sylvester Goodwin	2/24 shares
Daniel T. Samson	2/24 shares
Captain Benjamin S. Briggs, master of the vessel	8/24 shares

The *Mary Celeste* was still brigantine rigged but her large, single topsail had been divided into upper and lower topsails for easier handling. Her hull had been extensively rebuilt and enlarged so that her new length was 103 feet and her breadth increased slightly to 25.7 feet. She now had two decks and measured 282.28 tons, nearly eighty-four tons more than when she was launched. All of these repairs had cost in excess of $10,000, an important figure in the light of subsequent events. For all practical purposes she was almost a new vessel. And the *Mary Celeste* was about to begin the voyage that would give her a place in history.

❖ 3 ❖

A Voyage, A Derelict, A Mystery

It was mid-October 1872 when the *Celeste's* new captain, Benjamin S. Briggs, arrived in New York from his home in Marion, Massachusetts to supervise the loading of cargo and to make final arrangements for the voyage. The brigantine lay at Pier 50 in the East River and she would take on 1,701 barrels of alcohol destined for Genoa, Italy. About ten days later the Captain's wife Sarah and their two-year-old daughter Sophia joined him for the voyage.

Captain Briggs had good reason to be concerned about the proper stowage of the cargo. In the era of the wooden sailing vessel there were three cargoes that were considered particularly dangerous — coal, hay and alcohol. And it is worthy of note that in 1872 the sailing vessel still monopolized the seas. One day while the *Mary Celeste* was loading, New York recorded 382 sailing vessels in its port while steamers totalled just fifty-eight.

One of these windships, also a brigantine and also Nova Scotia-built, was berthed several miles away from the *Celeste* at the Venango Yard in Hoboken. The *Dei Gratia* of 295 tons was built in Bear River, N.S. the previous year for George

Captain Benjamin Spooner Briggs, master of the *Mary Celeste*
Courtesy of Peabody Museum of Salem.

F. Miller, a Bear River merchant. She was taking on 81,126 gallons of petroleum and would sail to Gibraltar for orders as to her final destination. Within weeks the two brigantines would become indelibly linked in marine history.

In all ten persons would make up the *Mary Celeste's* complement. At thirty-seven Captain Benjamin Spooner Briggs was a competent and experienced master mariner like his father before him. Briggs had previously commanded the schooner *Forest King*, the barque *Arthur* and the brig *Sea Foam*. He had spent considerable time in the Mediterranean and frequently sailed into Gibraltar where he was well known. The United States Consul at Gibraltar, Horatio J. Sprague would later write:

> Briggs I had known for many years and he always bore a good character as a Christian and as an intelligent and active shipmaster.

In 1862 Briggs had married his childhood sweetheart Sarah Elizabeth Cobb and two children were born to the couple, Arthur in 1865 and Sophia Matilda in 1870. As Arthur was of school age in 1872 he was to stay at home with his grandparents while two-year-old Sophia would accompany her parents to Genoa.

Sarah Briggs was musically inclined. She was a member of her church choir in Marion and she brought on board the *Celeste* a melodeon and a selection of music books. On long voyages it was not uncommon to invite members of the crew aft for Sunday evening hymn sings. Then, during the long stays in harbor, captains and their families visited back and forth and the melodeon would provide an enjoyable source of entertainment.

The first mate of the *Celeste* was Albert Richardson of Maine. He was twenty-eight years of age and had previously sailed with Captain Briggs. Richardson's wife was the niece of Mrs. J.H. Winchester, wife of the principal owner of the *Mary Celeste*. The second mate was Andrew Gilling, a twenty-five-year-old New Yorker while the cook-steward was Edmund

William Head. Head was twenty-three, also from New York and had married just before the vessel sailed.

Little is known of the four seamen signed on for the Genoa passage. They were Volkert and Box Lorenzen, Arian Martens and Gottlieb Goodschaad or Goodschall. All were Prussians and later information from Prussia indicated that they were 'peaceable and first-class sailors.' Certainly Briggs was satisfied. In their final letters to Briggs' mother before sailing Sarah had written:

> Benj. thinks we have got a pretty peaceable set (crew) this time all around if they continue as they have begun. Can't tell yet how smart they are.

In Captain Briggs' letter to his mother, written on November 3, there was a note of optimism:

> Our vessel is in beautiful trim and I hope we shall have a fine passage, but as I have never been in her before can't say how she'll sail.

On Tuesday morning, November 5, a tug towed the *Mary Celeste* away from the pier but as there was thick fog and a strong headwind Briggs decided to anchor off Staten Island. Two days later, on the morning of November 7, the weather being favorable the *Celeste* sailed to her meeting with destiny.

As the *Mary Celeste* sailed out of New York Harbor the *Dei Gratia* was readying for her own departure. She was under the command of David Reed Morehouse, a native of Sandy Cove, N.S. While only thirty-four years of age he had already been a master mariner for thirteen years and was regarded as an expert navigator. The mate who would play an integral role in the events to follow was Oliver Deveau of St. Mary's Bay, N.S., an experienced officer. A week and a day after the *Mary Celeste's* departure the *Dei Gratia* cleared New York for Gibraltar. Her name in translation means 'By Grace of God.'

Thus the two brigantines were sailing eastward across an Atlantic ocean which during any late fall season tends to be tempestuous and during the November of 1872 was unusually stormy. Vessel after vessel arriving in ports along the eastern seaboard of Canada and the United States reported continuous gale force winds and violent seas. It is known that for more than a week the *Dei Gratia* made heavy weather of it and it is highly probable that the *Mary Celeste* experienced the same conditions.

In the early afternoon of December 4 shore time and December 5 sea time (sea days began at 12:00 noon) Captain Morehouse of the *Dei Gratia* was keeping the deck with a seaman at the wheel. They sighted a vessel off the port bow about four or five miles distant. The stranger was sailing on a course approximately northwest by north, nearly opposite to that of the *Dei Gratia* which was sailing in a southeast by east direction. Morehouse studied the vessel through his glass. He was puzzled by the fact that no one appeared to be at the wheel and the vessel was obviously not under control. He sailed the *Dei Gratia* closer and hailed the stranger but received no response. Captain Morehouse then ordered his two mates, Oliver Deveau and John Wright along with seaman John Johnson to board the silent vessel and investigate. The three men put off in the *Dei Gratia's* boat about 3:00 p.m. and rowed to the vessel through the heavy seas. Johnson remained to tend the small boat while Deveau and Wright clambered on board. What they discovered would spark one of the enduring mysteries of the sea.

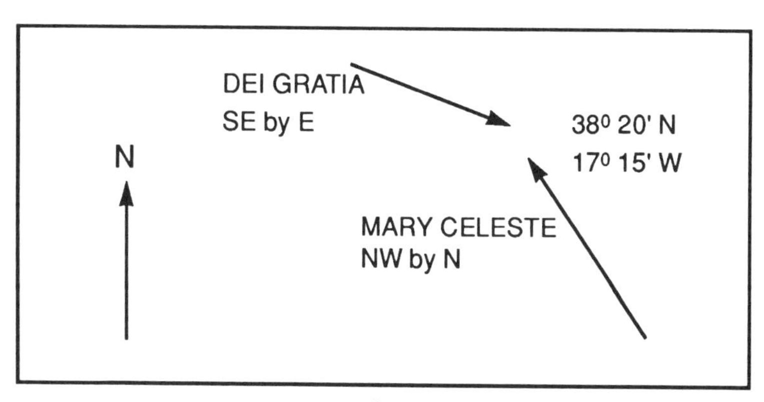

Captain David Reed Morehouse, master of *Dei Gratia*.
Courtesy of Peabody Museum of Salem.

The vessel, brigantine like the *Dei Gratia*, bore the name *Mary Celeste* of New York on her stern and a thorough search determined that not a soul was on board. The ship's chronometer, sextant, navigation book and the ship's papers were missing as was the one small boat which had been lashed across the main hatch.

Two sails, the foresail and upper topsail had blown away. Three sails were set, the jib, foretopmast staysail and forelower topsail. The remaining sails were properly furled except for the main staysail which had been hauled down and was lying loose on the forward house. The standing rigging was old but in good order but some of the running rigging had carried away and parts were hanging over the vessel's sides. And, as Oliver Deveau would later testify, 'THE MAIN PEAK HALYARD WAS BROKE AND GONE.'

On deck the two mates found both the fore and lazarette hatches open but the main hatch was closed and battened down. The binnacle, a wooden stand supporting the compass, had been knocked down and the compass broken. The wheel had not been lashed which accounted for the vessel's yawing when first sighted by the *Dei Gratia.*

In the after cabin the men found the *Mary Celeste's* log in the mate's quarters and the log slate, a temporary working log, on the cabin table. There had been a lot of water in the cabin, probably coming in through an open skylight and through an open door. Most of the water had run out but everything in the cabin including clothing and bedding remained wet. The cabin windows were covered over with canvas and boards indicating that the brigantine had been prepared for rough weather. The captain's berth had the appearance of a child having slept on it and articles of child's clothing and toys were scattered about the unmade berth. Nearby was Mrs. Briggs' sewing machine and melodeon along with her box of sewing articles, needles, thread, thimbles and buttons. The captain's charts and books were in the cabin, some in two bags under the berth. Also under the berth Deveau found an old sword which Captain Briggs had picked up as a souvenir on an earlier voyage to Italy. There

Brigantine *Dei Gratia*,.
Courtesy of Peabody Museum of Salem.

was no food or drink on the cabin table.

In the forward house the men found about a foot of water sloshing about the galley, held in by the high coaming under the open galley door. The stove was knocked out of place and there was no heat in it nor food on it. The kitchen utensils had all been washed and were in their proper places. The forecastle housed four berths and all of the bedding was damp. The seamen's clothing, oilskins, boots, even their pipes were in place suggesting a hasty departure. The storeroom contained sufficient provisions for six months and there was plenty of drinking water in the water casks lashed on deck. No wine, beer or spirits of any kind were found on board.

The vessel's pumps were in working order but there was about three and a half feet of water in the hold. Deveau and Wright suspected most of this water had come in through the open hatches as the hull appeared to be in good condition, in fact almost new. The cargo seemed to be well stowed with no visible damage to any of the barrels and there was no sign of any damage from a fire or explosion.

Lastly, there was the final entry on the vessel's log slate. It read:

> Monday, November 25. At 8 Eastern Point bore S.S.W. 6 miles distant.

This would have been the eastern point of Santa Maria or St. Mary's Island in the Azores Group. The vessel's position at that time was calculated to be 37°01'N, 25°01'W. When the *Dei Gratia* first sighted the derelict her position was 38°20'N, 17°15'W. Hydrographers later estimated that the *Mary Celeste* had sailed some 378 miles on her lonely way.

When the men returned to the *Dei Gratia* there was a hurried consultation with Captain Morehouse. The mates rather optimistically estimated the value of the *Mary Celeste's* cargo at about $80,000 so there was promise of a substantial reward for salvaging the vessel. Morehouse appreciated this factor but it was now December in the North Atlantic and he was mindful of his responsibility to his own vessel. The *Dei*

Oliver Deveau, First Mate of the *Dei Gratia*.
Courtesy of Peabody Museum of Salem.

Gratia's crew numbered only eight and to spare even the bare minimum necessary to man the *Celeste* would leave both vessels shorthanded. And there was still 600 miles of ocean to sail before reaching Gibraltar. In the end, however, he agreed to the salvage operation and directed mate Deveau along with seamen Charles Lund and Augustus Anderson to bring the abandoned brigantine into Gibraltar.

Oliver Deveau was a good man for the challenge ahead. A big, fearless and knowledgeable seaman, he held a mate's certificate and at one time had commanded a brig. He was also eager to undertake the adventure. The three took some cooked provisions, the mate's own navigation instruments and his personal watch as the cabin clock in the *Celeste* had been damaged by water. It was nearly dusk when they rowed over to the derelict in the *Dei Gratia's* small boat.

The three men immediately set to work, pumping out the water in the hold, closing hatches and doors, and rigging a temporary foresail. After some three hours of hard work they managed to get sail on the brigantine and lay a course for Gibraltar. It is likely that about this time Captain Morehouse made an entry in the log of the *Dei Gratia:*

> December 5. Begins with a fresh breeze and clear, sea still running heavy but wind moderating. Saw a sail to the E. 2 p.m. Saw she was under very short canvas, steering very wild and evidently in distress. Hauled up to speak her and render assistance, if necessary. At 3 p.m. hailed her and getting no answer and seeing no one on deck ... out boat and sent the mate and two men on board, sea running high at the time. He boarded her without accident and returned in about an hour and reported her to be the *Mary Celeste*, at and from New York, for Genoa, abandoned with 3½ ft. of water in hold ...

The two vessels were able to sail in company with each other until December 11 when they were nearing the northwest coast of Africa and approaching the Strait of Gibraltar. Then, about mid-afternoon, it came on to blow hard with heavy rain and in the poor visibility the two vessels lost sight of each other. Under the circumstances of weather conditions and being shorthanded, Deveau did not dare to attempt the passage into the Bay of Gibraltar. Instead he hove to under the Ceuta Light some thirty-five miles to the eastward along the Moroccon coast. The next day the *Mary Celeste* sailed back up the coast and reached Gibraltar on Friday, December 13 to find the *Dei Gratia* had entered port the previous evening.

Deveau and his two seamen were exhausted. They had labored long and hard to make the brigantine seaworthy and they had sailed her for a week with almost no rest culminating in the difficult feat of bringing the vessel through the last storm. Deveau wrote his wife:

> My men were all done out when I got in here, and I think it will be a week before I can do anything, for I never was so tired in my life. I can hardly tell what I am made of, but I do not care as long as I got in safe. I shall be well paid, for the *Mary Celeste* ... was loaded with alcohol and her cargo is worth eighty thousand dollars besides the vessel.

Deveau's hopes of being 'well-paid' were not to be. Immediately on arrival the *Mary Celeste* was taken into custody by T.J. Vecchio, Marshal of the Vice-Admiralty Court in Gibraltar. On December 18, 1872 the Court began its hearing 'on the claims of David Reed Morehouse, Master of the British brigantine *Dei Gratia* and for the Owners, Officers and Crew of the said brigantine as salvors.' The hearing would become a long, drawn-out affair with a most unsatisfactory conclusion.

❖ 4 ❖

The Vice-Admiralty Court

When the Court sat for its first sessions the presiding officer was Sir James Cochrane, Knight, Judge and Commissary of the Vice-Admiralty Court of Gibraltar. The other principals included: Frederick Solly Flood, Advocate and Proctor for the Queen and Henry Peter Pisani, Advocate and Proctor for David Reed Morehouse, Master of the British brigantine *Dei Gratia* and for her owners, officers and crew. The title Advocate and Proctor simply referred to lawyers with a particular expertise in marine affairs.

From the very beginning and for reasons of his own it was readily apparent that Frederick Solly Flood was determined to establish that revenge, murder or some other form of violence had occurred on board the *Mary Celeste*. It was his relentless pursuit of this line of reasoning that drew the hearings to unnecessary lengths and undoubtedly fueled the rather bloodthirsty theories advanced by some writers in later years.

Oliver Deveau was the first witness and he described in detail the state of the derelict when he and the second mate had boarded her. In describing the run into Gibraltar Deveau stated that the *Celeste* had leaked very little, that she was 'only a fair sailer' and that on the way they had spoken to a brigantine bound for Boston.

When questioned about the weather in the days immediately preceding the sighting of the *Mary Celeste* Deveau said that from November 15 to 24 the *Dei Gratia* had encountered stormy weather, 'most of the time very heavy weather.' During that period the only opportunity they had to ventilate their own cargo was about one hour when the main hatch was opened.

Since weather conditions in the days preceding the sighting of the *Mary Celeste* may well have played an important role in the vessel's abandonment, author Charles Edey Fay pursued the matter many years later. On May 27, 1940 he received a letter from Lieut. Col. J. Agostinho, Director of the Meteorological Service in the Azores stating:

> From the records from Angra do Heroismo and Ponta Delgada — the only two stations existing in 1872 — it is concluded that stormy conditions prevailed in the Azores on November 24 and 25, 1872. A cold front passed Angra do Heroismo between 3 and 9 p.m. on the 25th, the wind shifting then from S.W. to N.W. The minimum of pressure was 72 mm. and the wind velocity attained to 62 km. at Ponta Delgada at 9 p.m. on the 24th. Calm or light wind prevailed on the forenoon of the 25th but later became a gale force.

Oliver Deveau's own theory which he presented to the Court was that the crew of the *Celeste* sounded the pumps, found three and a half feet of water in the hold and thinking the vessel had developed a serious leak abandoned her. He said the pumps would normally be sounded every two to four hours in order to make the usual entry in the log, 'pumps carefully attended to.' He also noted:

> The fact that the men's clothing was all left behind along with their oilskins, boots and their pipes suggest they left in a great hurry. A sailor would generally take such things

especially his pipe if he was not in great haste.

After Deveau the other men who had been aboard the *Mary Celeste* also testified. Their descriptions as to what was found on the *Celeste* and the passage to Gibraltar differed little from that of Deveau. Meanwhile two other events worthy of mention did take place.

On December 23 the *Dei Gratia*, which had been in port since arriving on December 12, cleared Gibraltar for Genoa to deliver her cargo and collect the freight money. Oliver Deveau was in command while Captain Morehouse remained in Gibraltar, presumably to collect the salvage money when it was awarded. This action did not find favor with the presiding officer, Sir James Cochrane:

> The conduct of the salvors in going away as they have done is most reprehensible. Very strange why the captain of the *Dei Gratia*, who knows little to help the investigation should have remained here, whilst the first mate and crew who boarded the *Celeste* and brought her here should have been allowed to go away.

This resulted in Deveau having to leave the *Dei Gratia* in Genoa and return for a further appearance before the Court.

The statements of Deveau and other seamen from the *Dei Gratia* that the *Mary Celeste* was a 'fit and sound vessel' along with the departure of Deveau for Genoa further strengthened the suspicions of Frederick Solly Flood. He ordered and personally attended an exhaustive survey of the *Celeste* particularly looking for clues to substantiate his theories of violence. When the results were not to his liking he ordered a second survey but the outcome was no different. Flood then turned his attention to Captain Briggs' sword, convinced that the rust spots on the blade were bloodstains. A Gibraltar chemist examined the weapon and concluded the spots were not bloodstains. This infuriated Flood and he kept the chemist's report sealed and hidden for fourteen years.

The hearings had adjourned on December 21, 1872 then

resumed on January 29, 1873. This time Captain J.H. Winchester had arrived from New York to claim his vessel. He brought with him a new captain for the *Celeste*, George W. Blatchford of Massachusetts for Winchester was anxious to get his brigantine and her cargo on to Genoa. Frederick Solly Flood, ever suspicious, wanted Winchester to guarantee all claims against the vessel by her salvors, guarantee the costs of the Court and even any claims by the missing complement of the *Celeste* if they should ever turn up alive. Flood was insinuating to the Court and by letter to the British Board of Trade in London that someone had paid the seamen of the *Celeste* to murder their officers and to leave the vessel and cargo intact in a pre-determined place off the Azores where she would be 'discovered' by salvors.

Winchester was furious but also felt he was in some danger of being arrested by the Court so he abruptly left Gibraltar and returned to New York leaving Captain Blatchford to await the vessel's release.

The hearings dragged on into March when Deveau was recalled from Genoa for further testimony but he could add little to his previous statements. On March 10, after eighty-seven days in detention, the *Mary Celeste* sailed for Genoa. Five days later, March 15, 1873, there was a formal announcement in Gibraltar:

> In the Vice-Admiralty Court yesterday, the Hon. the Chief Justice gave judgment in the *Mary Celeste* salvage case, and awarded the sum of £1700 to the master and crew of the Nova Scotian brigantine *Dei Gratia* for the salvage services rendered by them: the costs of the suit to be paid out of the property salved. The *Mary Celeste* was valued at $5,700 and her cargo at $36,943 so that the award may be set down as one-fifth of the total value. The Judge further thought it right to express the disapprobation of the Court as to the conduct of the master of the *Dei Gratia* in allowing the first mate, Oliver Deveau, to do away with the vessel which had rendered

> necessary the analysis of the supposed spots or stains of blood found on the sword, and his Lordship also decided that the costs of the analysis should be charged against the amount awarded to the salvors.

In U.S. dollars the award amounted to about $8,300 so by the time it was divided among the owners and crew of the *Dei Gratia* no one got very much. Oliver Deveau's words to his wife when he wrote her on arrival in Gibraltar, 'I shall be well paid,' must have taken on a rather hollow tone when he received his share of the actual reward.

The aspersions cast on Captain Morehouse in the Court's decision seem unwarranted. He may well have sent the *Dei Gratia* on to Genoa on the orders of the vessel's owners. In any case he was acting on behalf of the owners in Gibraltar and would have the authority to receive any salvage money awarded by the Court. As to his character there has been nothing to indicate that he was anything but an honorable man.

The extraordinarily long Court hearings solved nothing except that the salvors received far less than a fair and just reward and that the characters of men like Morehouse and Winchester were put to question. Also, the energetic and ongoing suspicions of Frederick Solly Flood would continue to stimulate bizarre stories about the *Mary Celeste* for more than a century to come.

❖ 5 ❖

One Theory — Many Misconceptions

When the known facts concerning the *Mary Celeste*, her captain, the crew and the cargo are examined it is possible to develop a logical theory relative to the disappearance of her company.

After the brigantine arrived in Genoa and her cargo was discharged, it was found that there had been some leakage of alcohol altogether amounting to nine empty barrels. Whether or not the leakage occurred before the date of abandonment is not known but it is reasonable to assume that it had been a slow, ongoing process throughout most of the voyage. There is no doubt Captain Briggs would have been mindful of the volatile nature of his cargo and the need for regular ventilation. However, he would have been prevented from airing the cargo because of the adverse weather conditions for many days prior to November 25. It is also known that calm weather prevailed on the morning of the 25th. This presented Briggs with the first opportunity to ventilate the cargo and since the vessel's small boat lay across the main hatch, he ordered the fore hatch to be opened. As this was being done there could well have been an uprush of vapor from the hold perhaps with loud rumbling sounds that created fear in all on board of an imminent explosion.

This is essentially the basic theory held by such men as Dr. Oliver W. Cobb, a relative of Briggs and described as the dean of *Mary Celeste* chroniclers, by Charles Edey Fay who made a lifelong study of the incident and by several contemporary seafarers including Captain George D. Spicer.

Captain David Reed Morehouse agreed with this substance of the theory with a slight variation. He speculated that after the *Celeste* passed the eastern point of Santa Maria there was increased pressure on the leaking alcohol due to the warmer temperatures of the Azores. This caused fumes to suddenly invade the cabins and Briggs to immediately see that all doors and the cabin skylight were opened as well as the fore hatch.

Be that as it may any uprush of vapor along with possible rumbling sounds and the captain would instantly turn his attention to the safety of his family and the men. The next step in the theory is that he ordered the ship's boat launched and a coil of rope to be broken out to use as a long towline. Spare rope was normally stored in the lazarette and the men may have started to get the rope then decided to use the main peak halyard. It would have been but a minute's work to pull the halyard through its various blocks and it offered a line of some 300 feet in length. Then in order to slow the vessel's progress there was a hasty and careless reduction of sail which might account for the main staysail being found loose on top of the forward house.

While these preparations were under way Captain Briggs gathered together his chronometer, sextant and navigation book and ordered everyone into the ship's boat. The little boat, dangerously overloaded and with little freeboard, was now towing behind the brigantine while the captain awaited developments.

Those developments came hours later when the calm breeze of the morning gave way quickly to gale force winds. Although the *Mary Celeste* was under reduced sail she would have gathered speed rapidly as the wind rose either causing the towline to part or causing a chafing action where the line came around a stanchion. In his testimony in Gibraltar Oliver Deveau had stated that the main peak halyard 'was broke and gone.' In any event the small boat so heavily laden would not last long in the stormy seas. Perhaps it was dragged under, perhaps it capsized but its people did perish. The *Mary Celeste* continued by herself on an unsteady course until she was found by the *Dei Gratia.*

Possibly never in seafaring history have so many preposterous and bizarre stories been advanced concerning a ship's disaster. All of these fallacies indicate a complete disregard for the known facts concerning the captain, his officers and crew and the circumstances in which the vessel was found.

One of the more popular anecdotes, repeated time and again, was that still-warm oatmeal, bacon, eggs and coffee were found on the cabin table and a warm pillow lay on the captain's berth where the baby had slept. Twelve years later, in 1884, A. Conan Doyle, the creator of Sherlock Holmes, wrote a fanciful tale in *Cornhill Magazine* under an assumed name. In his story Doyle named the vessel *Marie Celeste* and whether it was intentional or not many have used this name ever since.

Another well-used theme, no doubt sparked by the suspicions of Gibraltar Advocate, Frederick Solly Flood, was one of mutiny. This theory in particular goes against everything that is known of the people on board the *Celeste.* And even if there had been a mutiny surely there would have been left some signs of a struggle, some signs of bloodshed. There were none. A book published in 1929 suggested that the whole affair was a hoax, that the two captains involved had conspired in order to share the salvage rewards. This idea is contrary to the indisputable documented evidence concerning the character of the two men and the fact that they were unknown to each other.

There were some over the years who suggested that an iceberg bearing down on the brigantine and threatening to sink her had forced the *Celeste's* people to take to the small boat only to be capsized in the heavy seas. The Amcrican Hydrographic Office ruled out this possibility due to the long drift of an iceberg in relatively warm waters before it could even reach the region of the Azores.

Another rather imaginative yarn is less well-known and did not become public until 1913. In summary it is told by a seaman named Demetrius:

> When the *Mary Celeste* was off the Azores she sighted a brig. As the two vessels came closer the brig hoisted the British ensign and signalled, 'Short of Provisions. Starving.' Captain Briggs had the Stars and Stripes raised and signalled, 'Send a boat.' A boat came alongside the *Celeste* with a swarthy, bearded man at the tiller. A tarpaulin covered what the *Celeste's* crew believed were empty cases to hold food from their stores. Suddenly the tarpaulin was pulled aside and six or seven armed men appeared and climbed aboard the *Celeste*. All of the *Celeste's* people were taken aboard the strange vessel. She proved to be a slaver and fever had carried away half her crew. Then the *Mary Celeste's* people caught the fever and one by one they died and were thrown overboard. The brig was eventually run down and sunk by an Italian steamer. There was only one survivor — Mr. Demetrius.

Demetrius said he kept the story to himself for more than forty years feeling that few would believe him. He was right.

A Captain Henry Appleby who had previously carried alcohol in his own vessel had another opinion. He thought that the dunnage, the lumber used to brace the barrels of alcohol in the hold, was covered with ice when put aboard the *Mary Celeste*. As the ice melted it made a vapor with the fumes of the alcohol and the resulting explosion blew off the fore hatch cover. The captain, fearing a worse explosion, ordered everyone into the ship's boat and as they towed along behind the boat capsized. However, the United States Weather Office reported that at the time the *Mary Celeste* was loading in New

York the temperature ranged between 40^0 and 51^0 Fahrenheit, hardly low enough to cause freezing.

In the years following 1872 at least four men presented themselves as survivors of the *Mary Celeste*. None bore a name that was on the vessel's crew list and even more important, none of the claimants was able to accurately describe the vessel, especially below decks.

Then there were suggestions that belonged in the realm of the silly. One was that a huge octopus had come alongside, lifted its tentacles and plucked off every living soul. Another was that something caught the attention of those on board and everybody rushed to one side putting the vessel on her beam ends and throwing every living soul in the water. Nine adults and an infant capable of doing this to a vessel over 100 feet in length and capable of carrying hundreds of tons of cargo?

The reason for the disappearance of all on board the *Mary Celeste* will never be known for certain. Oliver Deveau and one of the *Dei Gratia's* sailors said in their testimony at Gibraltar:

> Here was a vessel fully provisioned with food and water, with hull, masts, spars and standing rigging in good shape, with only normal leakage and, with the exception of two sails blown away, fit to go around the world.

The truth lies with the sea itself and with the bones of the old vessel on the Reef of the Rochelais.

The loss of those on board the *Mary Celeste* was felt in various places. To Benjamin Briggs' mother the disappearance of her son and his family was but another blow. She had already lost her eldest son, Nathan, to yellow fever in the Gulf of Mexico. Her only daughter, Maria, had drowned in a shipwreck and not long after the *Mary Celeste* incident her son, Oliver, drowned in the Bay of Biscay.

Frances, the wife of mate Albert Richardson, never remarried. She lived in Brooklyn, New York as a widow for sixty-five years until her death at ninety-one in 1937.

It was early in 1873 before the parents of the two Lorenzen brothers learned of the loss of their sons. Boz was soon to be married and he left his fiancée to mourn.

Young Arthur Briggs had only the memories of a seven-year-old boy for his father, mother and baby sister. That and a few mementos sent home from the *Mary Celeste*, some clothing, a few toys and a melodeon which in other times had been such a source of joy.

❖ 6 ❖
The Last Years

After the long detention in Gibraltar Captain George Blatchford took the *Mary Celeste* to Genoa, discharged the alcohol and brought the vessel back to Boston where he arrived on September 1, 1873. Captain J.H. Winchester and the other owners of the *Celeste* had had enough. The vessel was put up for sale but there were no buyers for her in Boston. The owners then sent her to New York where she finally sold. Winchester estimated he had lost $8,000 on the brigantine from the time of purchase until he sold her.

The new owner was the firm of Cartwright and Harrison of New York and the company used her mostly in the West Indies trade. In August 1877 Captain George D. Spicer had brought the barque *J.F. Whitney* into New York from Rotterdam. On August 31 he wrote in his diary:

> Today I was on board the old brigantine *Mary Celeste* which used to be the *Amazon* that I sailed on for over two years.

Just that — no further mention. Always when he boarded a vessel he had once sailed on or commanded he had some comment, usually favorable, 'She was a fine vessel' or 'She was a good sailer.' But for the *Mary Celeste*, nothing. Just perhaps his memories of the vessel were not so fond.

In 1886, some years after Cartwright and Harrison had disposed of the *Mary Celeste*, Cartwright spoke of the vessel in an interview with the *New York World:*

> We owned her for five years and of all the unlucky vessels I ever heard of, she was the most unlucky. When we sold her we found we had lost some $5,000. Most of the time that we owned her she was in the general West Indies trade and sometimes she lost her deck load of molasses and sometimes she didn't, but generally she did. We sent her out to Montevideo with a cargo of lumber and of course she arrived there minus the deck load; but we got to expecting this. She had heavy weather, lost sails and spars, etc. There the captain got a charter for Mauritius to carry horses. He had dreadful weather off the Cape of Good Hope and arriving at Mauritius the few horses left alive were too ill to be worth anything. The captain then obtained a good charter to bring a freight from Calcutta. On the passage home he was taken sick. In consequence the brig (?) had to put into Saint Helena, where after a detention of three weeks the captain died, and the mate brought the brig (?) home. We next sent her to the coast of Africa, and on this voyage she lost $1,000. After this we kept her in the West Indies trade and at the end of five years were glad to sell her at a low figure.

The score against the vessel by the time Cartwright and Harrison sold her included the death of two captains while in command of her, sinking a brig in the Strait of Dover, the disappearance of her total complement off the Azores and a history of losing money for her owners. It is little wonder that she was sometimes described as 'bewitched' or a 'hoodoo vessel.' And her career was not yet over.

The last owners of the *Mary Celeste* were a Boston group headed by Wesley A. Gove and during the next few years they too lost money on the vessel. Then in 1884 the brigantine was in Boston loading a mixed cargo for Haiti. She was now under the command of Captain Gilman C. Parker and her manifest listed such items as: 4,000 pounds of butter, 150 barrels of flour, 30 bales of dry goods, 975 barrels of pickled herring, 125 casks of ale and 54 cases of women's high button shoes.

The *Mary Celeste* cleared Boston for Haiti on December 15, 1884. On January 3, 1885 she was nearing her destination, the capital city Port-au-Prince, in clear weather and with a fair breeze. Yet under these ideal conditions she was driven on a plainly visible reef marked on the chart as the Rochelais Bank. The old vessel had ended her last voyage.

It was clearly a shipwreck designed to defraud the insurance companies for the actual cargo, insured for $25,000, would prove to be almost worthless. The Rochelais Bank had been carefully chosen as the site for several reasons. It was in an isolated location for the American underwriters to conduct their usual investigations, the reef presented no problems for the officers and crew to get ashore in the small boat, and the coral would quickly tear the vessel to pieces.

The settlement where Captain Parker and his men landed was Miragoane, a town of shacks and huts some fifty miles to the westward of Port-au-Prince. Here Captain Parker came across an American Consular agent by the name of Mitchell who was not averse to making a little money without worrying about the means. After a brief discussion Parker sold the vessel and cargo to Mitchell for $500. Then Parker and his men made their way to Port-au-Prince and took passage for home. Once back in the United States the good captain quickly arranged to have his men shipped out on long outward-bound voyages. Parker had committed barratry, a fraudulent act which in those times could result in the death sentence if convicted. But he did not worry. There was no one available to tell the story. Meanwhile the insurance companies were facing claims for the full $25,000.

However, all of the painstaking planning to collect the insurance money eventually came to naught because of one man. He was Kingman Putnam, a marine surveyor and investigator who happened to be in Haiti to investigate a shipwreck about forty miles from the *Mary Celeste*. The underwriters of the *Celeste* and her cargo asked Putnam to look into their case.

He went to Port-au-Prince, visited the consignees of the *Celeste's* cargo and obtained from them a listing of what they expected to receive in the vessel's cargo. At Miragoane he contacted Mitchell and found that the consular agent had saved most of the brigantine's cargo. Putnam later reported:

> I opened one case which had been shipped as cutlery and insured for $1,000. It contained dog collars worth about $50. Cases insured as shoes contained shoddy rubbers worth about 25 cents each.

That evening he arranged for a friend he knew to buy some of these cases from Mitchell and obtain from him a consular certificate stating that the packages were part of the *Mary Celeste's* cargo. The friend complied and the cases were sent on to a lawyer in Boston.

As a result Captain Parker was indieted for conspiracy and barratry and the shippers of the false cargo were indicted for conspiracy. Boston detectives investigating the shippers found that the fish that had been shipped was rotten and the casks of ale were the rinsings of old casks.

Parker was unquestionably guilty of both conspiracy and barratry but a hung jury and some peculiar maneuverings within the trial eventually allowed him to go free. The shippers confessed to conspiracy, were fined and within six months all were out of business. Captain Gilman Parker never obtained another command. He eked out a meagre living doing various menial jobs before dying a pauper in 1891.

The strange career of the *Mary Celeste* had finally come to an end. She had cost lives and money and there was little that could be placed on her credit side.

As for her builder, Joshua Dewis continued to farm and lumber and he built two more vessels. On the shore of his farm property there is a hollow in the land running down to Fundy's waters. In this secluded spot he set up a shipyard and in 1865 launched the 365 ton brig *Albert Dewis*. The brig was followed in 1869 by the 579 ton barque *G.P. Payzant*. The last vessel built in Joshua's yard was the barque *Advocate* of 635 tons but this time the builder was Ebenezer Bigelow of Canning, N.S.

Dewis had more contributions to make to the burgeoning shipbuilding industry. His eldest son, Robert, became a master mariner and commanded several square-riggers before he too turned to building vessels. Joshua's eldest daughter, Emma, married Ebenezer Cox of Kingsport, one of Nova Scotia's foremost shipbuilders. And Margaret, the third child, married William Henry Bigelow, a businessman in Spencers Island who was very much involved with shipbuilding in that locality. Joshua died on May 21, 1896 at the age of eighty-one. During his lifetime the building of wooden sailing vessels in Nova Scotia had moved from relative infancy to its greatest years and by the 1890s was settling into its long sunset.

The Dewis farm, now in other hands, still commands one of the finest views along the Parrsboro shore. Soon it will overlook the entrance to the vast new wilderness park on Cape Chignecto.

There is one last aftermath to the saga of the *Mary Celeste*. Just sixty-one years and twenty-six days after the *Celeste* drove on the Reef of The Rochelais, on January 29, 1946, another famous Nova Scotia vessel with an entirely different history died on a reef not far from the old brigantine. She was the schooner *Bluenose*.

Epilogue

Experts examining the remnants of a wreck found off Haiti in 2001 are convinced that they belong to the *Mary Celeste*. Thus while the final resting place of the old vessel may indeed be established, the mystery surrounding the disappearance of her complement of ten in 1872 remains.

❖ Bibliography ❖

Bradford, G. *The Secret of the* ***Mary Celeste***. Barre, Mass.: Barre Publishing Company, 1966.

Bryan, George S. *Mystery Ship (The* ***Mary Celeste*** *In Fancy And In Fact)*. New York: J.B. Lippincott Company, 1942.

Campbell, Bertha. *History of Advocate*. Amherst, N.S.: Amherst Citizen, A Series of Articles, 1988.

Campbell, Frank W. *Canada Post Offices 1755-1895*. Boston: Quartermain Publications, Inc., 1972.

Fay, Charles Edey. ***Mary Celeste.*** *The Odyssey Of An Abandoned Ship*. Salem, Mass.: Peabody Museum, 1942.

Jephcott, C.M. et al. *The Postal History of Nova Scotia and New Brunswick, 1754-1867*. Toronto: Sissins Publications Ltd., 1964.

Lockart, J.G. *A Great Sea Mystery*. London: Philip Allan and Co. Ltd., 1927.

Monro, Alexander. *New Brunswick With A Brief Outline of N.S. and P.E.I.*. Halifax: John Nugent, 1855.

Raddall, Thomas H. *Footsteps On Old Floors.* Garden City, New York: Doubleday and Company, Inc., 1968.

Spicer, Lottie. *Spencers Island And A History of Our Spicer Ancestors.* Spencers Island: Typescript, Undated.

AND

Verbatim Report — Court of Inquiry Into The Abandonment of the *Mary Celeste.*

Letters to the author from Charles Edey Fay and Dr. Chester Cobb, 1950s.

Letters and Diaries, Captain George D. Spicer, Spencers Island, various years.

Census of Nova Scotia — Taken on March 30, 1861.

Family Records, The Dewis Family.

Various newspapers, various years.